Dear Parents and Educators,

Welcome to Penguin Young Readers! As parents and educators, you know that each child develops at his or her own pace—in terms of speech, critical thinking, and, of course, reading. Penguin Young Readers recognizes this fact. As a result, each Penguin Young Readers book is assigned a traditional easy-to-read level (1–4) as well as a Guided Reading Level (A–P). Both of these systems will help you choose the right book for your child. Please refer to the back of each book for specific leveling information. Penguin Young Readers features esteemed authors and illustrators, stories about favorite characters, fascinating nonfiction, and more!

Pearl and Wagner: Three Secrets

LEVEL **3**

GUIDED READING LEVEL **K**

This book is perfect for a **Transitional Reader** who:
- can read multisyllable and compound words;
- can read words with prefixes and suffixes;
- is able to identify story elements (beginning, middle, end, plot, setting, characters, problem, solution); and
- can understand different points of view.

Here are some **activities** you can do during and after reading this book:
- Venn Diagram: Pearl and Wagner are good friends. Think about how they are alike and how they are different. Then, on a separate piece of paper, draw a Venn diagram—two circles which overlap. Label one circle "Pearl" and the other circle "Wagner." Write the character traits that are specific to each character in the parts of the circles that don't touch. Write the character traits they share in the space where the circles overlap.
- Make Connections: Have you ever kept a secret for a friend? How did it feel? Wagner says, "Secrets are too hard to keep." Do you agree?

Remember, sharing the love of reading with a child is the best gift you can give!

—Bonnie Bader, EdM
    Penguin Young Readers program

*Penguin Young Readers are leveled by independent reviewers applying the standards developed by Irene Fountas and Gay Su Pinnell in *Matching Books to Readers: Using Leveled Books in Guided Reading*, Heinemann, 1999.

For Bob, who created the
world's greatest Zoomer—KM

For Chuck and Jeffrey,
my third-grade pals—RWA

Penguin Young Readers
Published by the Penguin Group
Penguin Group (USA) Inc., 375 Hudson Street, New York, New York 10014, USA
Penguin Group (Canada), 90 Eglinton Avenue East, Suite 700, Toronto, Ontario M4P 2Y3, Canada
(a division of Pearson Penguin Canada Inc.)
Penguin Books Ltd, 80 Strand, London WC2R 0RL, England
Penguin Ireland, 25 St Stephen's Green, Dublin 2, Ireland (a division of Penguin Books Ltd)
Penguin Group (Australia), 707 Collins Street, Melbourne, Victoria 3008, Australia
(a division of Pearson Australia Group Pty Ltd)
Penguin Books India Pvt Ltd, 11 Community Centre, Panchsheel Park, New Delhi—110 017, India
Penguin Group (NZ), 67 Apollo Drive, Rosedale, Auckland 0632, New Zealand
(a division of Pearson New Zealand Ltd)
Penguin Books (South Africa), Rosebank Office Park, 181 Jan Smuts Avenue,
Parktown North 2193, South Africa
Penguin China, B7 Jiaming Center, 27 East Third Ring Road North,
Chaoyang District, Beijing 100020, China

Penguin Books Ltd., Registered Offices: 80 Strand, London WC2R 0RL, England

Text copyright © 2004 by Kate McMullan. Illustrations copyright © 2004 by R. W. Alley. All rights
reserved. First published in 2004 by Dial Books for Young Readers, an imprint of Penguin Group
(USA) Inc. Published in 2013 by Penguin Young Readers, an imprint of Penguin Group (USA) Inc.,
345 Hudson Street, New York, New York 10014. Manufactured in China.

The original art was created using pen and ink, watercolor, and a few colored pencils on Strathmore Bristol.

The Library of Congress has cataloged the Dial edition
under the following Control Number: 2002153680

ISBN 978-0-448-46472-5   10 9 8 7 6 5 4 3 2 1

PENGUIN YOUNG READERS

LEVEL 3
TRANSITIONAL
READER

Pearl and Wagner
Three Secrets

by Kate McMullan
pictures by R. W. Alley

Penguin Young Readers
An Imprint of Penguin Group (USA) Inc.

Contents

VISITORS:
CHECK IN
AT THE
OFFICE →

Lulu

BUD

Chapter 1

Ice Cream Secrets

Ms. Star's class was going to visit an ice cream factory.

"I love ice cream," said Pearl.

"I dream about it," said Wagner.

Everyone lined up for the bus.

"Save me a place, Wag," said Pearl.

She ran to get her jacket.

Lulu got in line behind Wagner.

"Want to know a secret?" she said.

"No," said Wagner.

"Secrets are too hard to keep."

But Lulu told him the secret, anyway.

Pearl came back.

She saw Lulu whispering to Wagner.

Pearl and Wagner sat down in the bus.

"What did Lulu say?" Pearl asked.

"I can't tell you," said Wagner.

"It's a secret."

"Oh," said Pearl.

Wagner felt awful.

The bus pulled up
to the ice cream factory.
"Wow!" said Henry.
"This place looks like
a giant ice cream cone!"
"Lulu won't mind if you tell me,"
said Pearl.
"I can't," said Wagner.
He felt even worse.

The class went inside.

They saw a large vat of cream.

Big paddles were stirring it.

"Oh boy!" said Bud.

"Did you promise not to tell?"

said Pearl.

"Not exactly," said Wagner.

A machine poured mint into
the cream.
Another machine added
chocolate chips.
"Yum!" said Henry.
"Then tell me," said Pearl.
"I shouldn't," said Wagner.

A machine poured the ice cream
into boxes.

The boxes went into a big freezer.

"Brrrr!" said Bud.

"Give me a hint," said Pearl.

"It wouldn't be right," said Wagner.

The last stop was the Tasting Room.

Everyone got a double-dip cone.

"Tell me the first word," said Pearl.

Wagner put his hands over his mouth.

He shook his head.

Lulu came by, licking her cone.

"Aren't you having any?" she asked.

"Wagner won't tell me your secret,"

said Pearl.

"I'm having a birthday party,"
said Lulu.

"That's not a secret!" said Pearl.

"I know about your party."

"Wagner didn't," said Lulu.

"It was a secret to him."

"Secrets," said Wagner.
"Phooey!"

"Time to go, class!" said Ms. Star.

"Wait!" said Wagner.

"I didn't look around."

"I didn't get any ice cream!"
said Pearl.

"Next time," said Ms. Star.

Everyone got back on the bus.
Pearl and Wagner could not believe
they had missed the ice cream.

"Don't worry," said Ms. Star.
"We have another class trip
next week."
"Where?" said Wagner.
"I'll keep that a secret," said Ms. Star.

Chapter 2

Wagner's Secret

Lulu sent everyone in the class an invitation.

"We will all ride the bumper cars,"
Lulu told everyone.
"We will all ride the tea cups.
We will all ride the Zoomer."

"What is the Zoomer?" asked Wagner.

"The Zoomer is a roller coaster,"

said Lulu.

"It is the biggest, fastest,

scariest roller coaster ever."

"Oh," said Wagner.

"I am wearing my new red hat
to Lulu's party,"
Pearl told Wagner at recess.
"What are you wearing?"

"I'm not going," said Wagner.

"WHAT?" said Pearl.

"Why not?"

"I have to get my teeth cleaned,"
said Wagner.

"You did that last week," said Pearl.

"I have to buy new socks,"
said Wagner.

"Tell me the real reason," said Pearl.

"It's a secret," said Wagner.

"I won't tell," said Pearl.

"I hate roller coasters," said Wagner.

"Have you ever been
on a roller coaster?" said Pearl.

Wagner shook his head.

"The cars go too high," he said.

"They come down too fast.
And they are way too loud."

"Lulu's party won't be any fun
without you, Wagner," said Pearl.
"I am going to help you.
When I am done,
you will love roller coasters."

"Don't count on it," said Wagner.

Pearl and Wagner climbed to the
top of the jungle gym.
"You are up high now," said Pearl.
"How do you feel?"
"Not bad," said Wagner.

Pearl took Wagner over to the slide.
"Slide down as fast as you can,"
she told him.

Wagner zoomed
down the slide.
"How do you feel?"
said Pearl.
"Fine," said Wagner.

Pearl took Wagner over to the fence.
Workers on the other side of it
were using a jack hammer.
RAT-A-TAT! RAT-A-TAT!

"THIS IS LOUD,"
Pearl yelled over the noise.
"HOW DO YOU FEEL?"
"DANDY!" yelled Wagner.

"One more thing," said Pearl.

"Say this to yourself over and over.

'I rule the roller coaster!'"

"I rule the roller coaster!"

said Wagner.

"Say it like you mean it," said Pearl.

Wagner said,

"I RULE THE

ROLLER COASTER!"

"Who rules?" said Pearl.

"ME!" said Wagner.

"I DO!"

"You're ready," said Pearl.

"Bring on the Zoomer!"

said Wagner.

Chapter 3
Pearl's Secret

On Saturday, Pearl and Wagner
went to Ride-o-Rama.

They gave their presents for Lulu
to Lulu's mom.

Then they ran to the bumper cars.

"Let's drive!" said Lulu.

Bam! Wagner bumped Bud.

Bam! Bud bumped Pearl.

Bam! Pearl bumped Lulu.

BAM! Lulu bumped Henry.

"Yikes!" said Henry.

"What fun!" yelled Lulu.

Everyone raced for the tea cups.

They got in and sat down.

The tea cups started spinning.

They spun faster and faster.

When the ride was over,

everyone was good and dizzy.

"To the Zoomer!" yelled Lulu.

Pearl and Wagner ran over
to the roller coaster.

"Who rules?" said Pearl.

"I do!" said Wagner.

"Pearl! Wagner!"
called Lulu.

"That is the Little Duck
roller coaster.

The Zoomer is over here!"

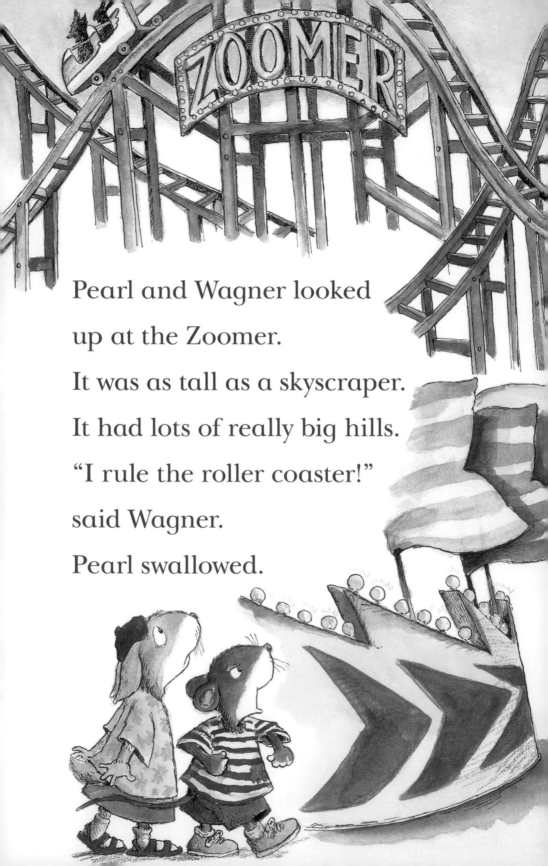

Pearl and Wagner looked
up at the Zoomer.
It was as tall as a skyscraper.
It had lots of really big hills.
"I rule the roller coaster!"
said Wagner.
Pearl swallowed.

Henry and Lulu got into a car.
A man pulled a bar down
in front of them.

Pearl and Wagner were next.
"I'm ready!" said Wagner.
"I'm not going," said Pearl.

"WHAT?" said Wagner.

"Why not?"

"I have to get a drink of water,"
said Pearl.

"You can do that later," said Wagner.

"My hat might fly off," said Pearl.

"Tell me the real reason,"
said Wagner.

"It's a secret," said Pearl.

"I won't tell," said Wagner.

"I'm scared!" said Pearl.

"Next!" called the man.

Wagner sat down in the car.

"Come on, Pearl," he said.

"I will help you."

Pearl sat down next to Wagner.

The man pulled the bar down
in front of them.

"Good-bye, Wagner," said Pearl.

"It's been nice knowing you."

"Let's zoom!" yelled Lulu.

The roller coaster

rolled up the first hill.

"I am going to be sick," said Pearl.

"I have a better idea," said Wagner.

"What?" said Pearl.

"Scream!" said Wagner.

The roller coaster raced
down the hill.
Pearl screamed.
Wagner screamed.
Everyone on the roller coaster
screamed like crazy.

They flew up the hills.

They shot down the hills.

They zoomed around the curves.

They raced down the track
and stopped.

The man lifted the bar.

"Over so soon?" said Wagner.

Pearl and Wagner got out of the car.

"Let's go again!" said Pearl.

Lulu looked a little green.

"Let's have presents first," she said.

Lulu opened her presents.
Then everyone sang
"Happy Birthday."
Lulu blew out seven
candles.

Pearl asked for three scoops
of ice cream on her cake.
"I love ice cream!" said Pearl.

"That's no secret," said Wagner.
He sang, "You scream, I scream,
we all scream for ice cream!"

After their cake,

the two friends rode the Zoomer

until it was time to go home.